MW00915917

HALLOWEEN NIGHT AT THE SPIDERS' PARTY

GLORIA GARDNER
Illustrated by Eric M. Strong

LUMINARE PRESS

WWW.LUMINAREPRESS.COM

Printed in the United States of America

Illustrations by Eric M. Strong

Luminare Press
442 Charnelton St.
Eugene, OR 97401
www.luminarepress.com

LCCN: 2021915429
ISBN: 978-1-64388-807-1

This book is dedicated to everyone who loves Halloween!

*It's the special time of the year when we get excited about the costumes,
the pumpkins, the spooky surprises, and the trick-or-treats.
Yes, we love it!*

*And did you ever wonder if it's only
kids and grownups who celebrate Halloween?*

Could there be others? You're in for a surprise!

*Find out what spiders and insects do when it's Halloween.
You may be the first to know!*

There were four little friends. Insect friends. Their names were Buzzy, Hopper, Glow and Beetle-Lee. Each one was special. One was a yellow jacket, one was a grasshopper, one was a firefly, and one was a beetle.

It was Halloween Day. All of the insect friends were excited and wanted to have fun.

"Let's have an adventure!" Hopper suggested.

"Where could we go? What could we do?"
Glow wondered.

"Maybe we could watch the Dragonfly Parade," Buzzy said.

"Or maybe we could listen to the Cricket Chorus," Hopper added.

"Or maybe we could see the Sowbug Somersault Contest," Glow said.

"Well, I've got the best idea of all," said Beetle-Lee, "let's go see the spiders, because they're having a Halloween party. I've even got a picture of their house."

"Yes!" they all said.

"But when? Now?" one of the friends asked.

"No, we'll wait 'til tonight, when it will be really dark and spooky," said Buzzy.

"Oh, this will be fun," said Hopper, "I mean, scary!"

"Let's do it," they all agreed.

"And let's bring a bag of nibbles along, in case we get hungry. We can pack it with good things to eat, like leaves and seeds and roots and flowers," Glow said.

"Perfect," said Buzzy, "I'll gather some and put them in a bag for you to carry, Hopper."

"Okay, as soon as the Halloween moon is in the sky, as soon as the kids in their costumes pass by, as soon as the witch on her broom starts to fly, then we'll go and peek in the Spider House," said Beetle-Lee."

So Buzzy, Hopper, Glow and Beetle-Lee began their adventure. They moved carefully along the path, each one right behind the other, with their eyes were wide open.

"Oh," said Beetle-Lee, "look at the big arms on the trees, and see how the shadows move and freeze."

"Oh," said Hopper, "listen to the owl hooting its sound, and see all the nuts that are on the ground, and feel the tangling weeds grab our legs all around."

"Look," said Glow, "we're almost there. Do you see the Spider House? Look how it's all decorated for Halloween."

"This is going to be exciting! Who's ready?" asked Buzzy.

"I am," said Hopper.

"Me, too," said Beetle-Lee and Glow.

"Let's get a little closer," said Hopper.

"Good, now we're here," said Beetle-Lee. "Can you see the spider at the window? It's a furry, black spider with big long legs. I think it's smiling at us. I think it's waving to us."

"Oh, I think so, too," said Buzzy. "Maybe, it's friendly."

"Why don't we go inside and have some Halloween fun?" said Beetle-Lee.

"Yes, I see the door is opening," said Glow, "let's see what the spiders have ready for us."

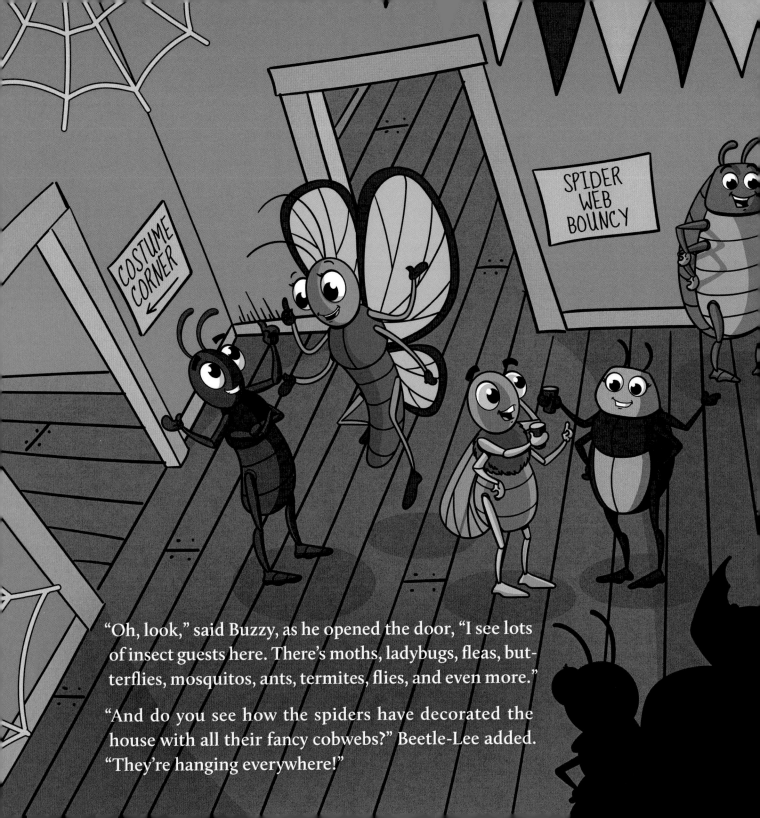

"Oh, look," said Buzzy, as he opened the door, "I see lots of insect guests here. There's moths, ladybugs, fleas, butterflies, mosquitos, ants, termites, flies, and even more."

"And do you see how the spiders have decorated the house with all their fancy cobwebs?" Beetle-Lee added. "They're hanging everywhere!"

"And look at all the games they have," added Hopper.

"I'm ready to try them all," said Beetle-Lee, "and I can't wait to get started."

"Me, too," Glow added, "it's going to be a really fun Halloween for us."

"There's a Costume Corner, right over there," Buzzy pointed out. "The spiders are putting costumes on the guests to dress them up like mummies."

"I want a mummy costume," said Beetle-Lee. "Come and watch how they put a mummy costume on me," he said.

"Oh, look," said Hopper, "they're wrapping threads around you." "How does it feel?" he asked.

"It feels funny. It's kind of tight," said Beetle-Lee. "Oh, oh, it's too tight. Now, it hurts me. I want out of this mummy costume, but the spiders won't let me out."

"Go ahead, Beetle-Lee, show them what you can do," said Glow. "Use your pinchers to pull the threads away, you can do it!"

"Look! I can do it!" said Beetle-Lee. "I can get out. See, I'm free! Good for me. Now I'm not a mummy anymore. And let's make sure that the other insects get free, too. They don't like the mummy costumes, either."

"Good for us, we did it!" they all said.

"Oh, look over here. There's a big bouncy. It's a spider web bouncy. Who wants to try it?" asked Buzzy.

"I do," said Hopper. "I'm a grasshopper, and I really like to bounce. Watch me, here I go. Bounce, bounce. This is fun for me! Bounce, bounce. I don't ever want to stop! But wait, some of the other insect guests look like they're getting stuck and tangled up in the spider web bouncy, and they're scared. Let's see what I can do to help them? I think I'm big enough to bounce really hard, but can you give me the bag of nibbles to hold while I'm bouncing? Then I'll be even heavier when I bounce, and I'll be strong enough to save the guests that are stuck. Oh, good! It works! Look at the bouncy now. It's breaking apart. The spider web is pulling apart. I'm glad that I'm such a good jumper. And can you help me get all the insects loose from the sticky threads?" Hopper asked.

"Here we come, we're all going to help you," they said.

"Oh, good for us, we've rescued all the bouncing insects," said Beetle-Lee, "and I'm glad we did!

"Oh, look over here," said Glow, "there's a Halloween Tickle Corner. Let's see who wants to try it."

"I do," said Buzzy, "it's fun to tickle, and I like to laugh. Watch me have fun!"

"Oh, look at the spiders tickling Buzzy and all the other guests. I think they like it. Oh-oh, maybe not. They're all trying to get away from the tickling spiders, but the spiders won't let them go. The spiders are trying to carry them away, and the insects don't like it," Beetle-Lee said.

"Buzzy, save yourself! Save everybody! You can do it!" said Hopper.

And just then, they heard Buzzy make his special noises, "Bzzz, bzzz, bzzz." And they knew that

Buzzy could also use his stinger, if he needed to, so that he could help protect all the insects.

"Good for you, Buzzy, you did it," said Glow. "That was smart. You saved everyone! And see, the spiders are letting go of all the insects. Now everyone is safe again."

"That's great!" said Beetle-Lee.

"Guess what I see?" asked Hopper. "Look over there. Do you see that?"

"Oh, there's a Mystery Tunnel. Do you want to see where it goes? What could the mystery be?" said Buzzy.

"Let me go down there," said Glow. "I'm a firefly, and I light up in the dark. It sure does look dark inside the tunnel, but I'm not afraid of the dark. Watch me go exploring."

"There she goes, crawling down deep in the tunnel," said Hopper.

"Oh, let's peek in there and see what Glow finds," said Beetle.

"Do you think that there's anything scary in there? Or is it just pretend scary?" said Buzzy.

"Oh-oh, did you see that? Look! Down there in the Mystery Tunnel, I can see Glow's firefly lights. Look at that! There is something very scary there. I can see a scary, monster spider," said Hopper.

"Glow, keep flashing your lights. You really surprised the monster spider. With your lights blinking in the tunnel, you can see everything you need to, and the monster spider can't catch you or any of the other insects by surprise. And you can even fly away to escape, and all the other insects can get out safely with your help," said Beetle-Lee.

"Good, here she comes! And she's got all the little insects, too. Hooray for Glow!" they all shouted.

"You were really brave, Glow," said Buzzy.

"I'm glad that I'm a firefly," Glow said proudly.

And then Hopper said, "Oh, look what the spiders are getting ready to do now. They're going to have a race."

"Can we be in the race, too? I can go fast", said Buzzy.

"Me, too"! they all said.

"Oh, the spiders are showing us where the race will be. It will be outside, all the way around the Spider House," Hopper said.

"I've got a good idea," said Buzzy, "come close, and I'll whisper the plan to you." Then after they all heard his idea, he added, "Does everyone know what to do?"

"We sure do!"
they all said.

"Get ready now.
Here we go!"
said Buzzy.

Everyone lined up at the starting line, and the race began.

All the spiders raced. And all the insect guests raced. And of course, the four friends raced, too. When they got to the end of the race, guess who won? The four friends! And even better than that, they kept right on racing, all the way home.

When they finally got back to their home, the four insect friends said, "Oh, we had fun tonight on Halloween, and those spiders never caught us, even though they played their best Halloween tricks on us. But we played our tricks, too. And we won! Happy Halloween!"

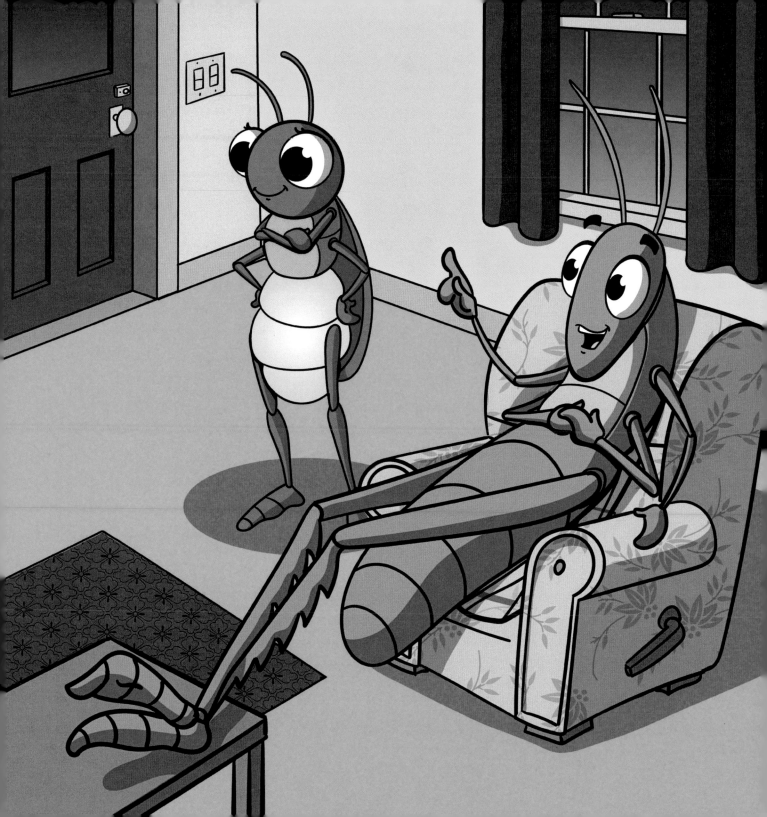

ABOUT THE AUTHOR

Gloria Gardner discovered her calling to become a teacher early on and graduated from U.C. Berkeley. She worked successfully in public schools for nine years as an elementary school teacher and then established a preschool, serving as director and teacher for thirty-eight years. She received a "Preschool Teachers Make A Difference" award. Gloria was a resident of California for many years, and now she is living happily in Oregon.

ABOUT THE ILLUSTRATOR

Eric lives to create narratives that help underdogs exceed their wildest dreams!

    With over 20 years of professional experience as a freelance artist he has worked on over 60 children's books, 400 animated videos, and thousands of professional illustrations. He has worked for many large companies but his favorite clients are self-publishing authors and small studios.

Made in the USA
Middletown, DE
26 September 2021